MW01118394

Puzzling ! Thrilling Mystery . Strangest Unsolved Mysteries of All Time.

Prabir RaiChaudhuri

Published by Prabir Rai Chaudhuri, 2022.

PUZZLING ! THRILLING MYSTERY . STRANGEST UNSOLVED MYSTERIES OF ALL TIME.

First edition. August 22, 2022.

Copyright © 2022 Prabir RaiChaudhuri.

ISBN: 979-8201394219

Written by Prabir RaiChaudhuri.

Also by Prabir RaiChaudhuri

Fantasy-Fun-Moral ; Selected short stories for kids with moral
Puzzling ! Thrilling Mystery . Strangest Unsolved Mysteries of All Time.
Manga, Anime sketch, drawing, coloring techniques

Watch for more at https://www.manusherbhasha.com/.

Table of Contents

Acknowledgements The author and publisher would like to thank all the friends and teachers who discussed this book in the early stages of its development. There are instances where we have been unable to trace or contact copyright holders . If notified, the publisher will be pleased to acknowledge the use of copyright material. Our main aim is to expand urge of investigation in mind of every people in the globe and clear the fear of unknown things. For doing so we have to go through several books and articles that help us to build this exceptional book that would be easy to read , understand and remember. . As a whole we composed the materials where it might be found some are same with large world of books like this . Our sincere apology to them if someone finds any material seems to be the same or nearly the same.

Greatest Unsolved Mysteries Of All Time

BY- PRABIR RAI CHAUDHURI

PREFACE

The discovery of science and advanced technology have advanced human civilization. The desire to know and discover has solved many unknown mysteries in the world, nature and even in the outer space. Today technology is so advanced that it seems that it can solve any mystery. But it is also surprising to think that there are already many incidents and issues, which have not been resolved for years. Despite the efforts of many wise people and scientists, there was no solution. Surprise. Isn't it? Let's take a look at the thrilling mysteries that still have no explanation. Will you give it a try? Read on to see what that mysteries are..

PART - 1
A brief history of "Unsolved Mysteries"

A man sits next to you on an airplane. He looks familiar — is he an amnesiac who's wandered miles from home?

A woman in line at the grocery store seems to be stealing furtive glances. Could she be the missing heir to a fortune . . . or a murderer?

Some people would call these paranoid thoughts. But this behavior probably seems pretty normal if you grew up watching "Unsolved Mysteries." The primetime show used creepy music, spooky lightning, and sometimes-questionable acting in an effort to crack vexing cases, both legal and metaphysical. Join us. Perhaps you can help solve a mystery—or at least dive into the mysteries behind "Unsolved Mysteries," a show about true crime before true crime was a mass media obsession, and reality television before reality television was everywhere.

Primetime crime

*I*n the mid-1980s, primetime television didn't leave a lot of room for reality programming. Aside from some Geraldo specials, shows about real people involved in crimes just weren't common. In fact, the closest thing viewers had ever seen to a reality-based crime show was a series called "Wanted" that aired on CBS for one season in 1955. "Wanted" featured real victims and law enforcement officials in a telecast that urged viewers to help them capture fugitives. It was likely the first program of its kind, but it wasn't popular, and the format went dormant for about 30 years.

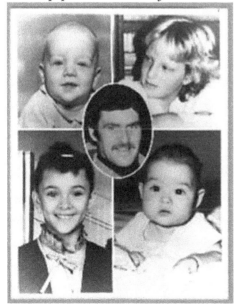

That fact didn't go unnoticed by producing partners John Cosgrove and Terry Dunn Meurer, who met while working at the same production company in the early 1980s. In 1985, they created a series of specials for NBC titled "Missing . . . Have You Seen This Person?" Hosted by "Family Ties" star Meredith Baxter and her then-husband David Birney, the specials profiled children and adults who had disappeared. At the time, the concept of "stranger danger" and kids profiled on milk cartons was in the cultural zeitgeist, and Cosgrove and Meurer believed a show exploring these types of cases could be something rare for primetime television — a public service.

They were right. The "Missing" specials resulted in 25 people being found and reunited with their families. They were also a ratings success for NBC. Cosgrove and Meurer knew they had something, but there were a few missing pieces.

For one thing, it was hard to continue doing specials based strictly on missing persons. While there was no shortage of cases, a solid hour of them might prove emotionally taxing for viewers. For another, even though the shows acted as a way to inform the public, they still had to be entertaining and hold the viewer's attention.

PUZZLING ! THRILLING MYSTERY . STRANGEST UNSOLVED MYSTERIES OF ALL TIME.

So Cosgrove and Meurer took a cue from a special they had produced for HBO back in 1983 called "Five American Guns." In the special, they had used reenactments to portray the far-reaching consequences of owning a handgun. If they could combine mysteries of all types with dramatic reenactments, they might have a shot at shaking up the primetime landscape. All they needed was a host.

The untouchable Robert Stack

O bviously, they chose Robert Stack. But not at first. Or second.

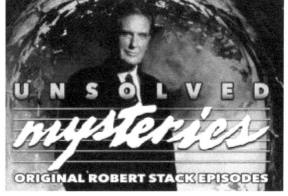

When "Unsolved Mysteries" premiered as a special on January 20, 1987, actor Raymond Burr was hosting. Burr is probably best known for playing Perry Mason, the dogged criminal defense lawyer who rarely lost a case over nine seasons (the guy was good).

Burr had an authoritative presence that lent itself well to stories of disappearances, unsolved murders, and lost loves. But Burr didn't return for the following specials. Those were hosted by actor Karl Malden, who won an Academy Award for his role in 1951's "A Streetcar Named Desire" opposite Marlon Brando. Malden did two of the specials before he also bowed out.

When "Unsolved Mysteries" returned for a fourth primetime special, there was a new host. His name was Robert Stack, and viewers knew him best as legendary lawman Eliot Ness in the popular 1960s drama "The Untouchables," which had just been turned into a major feature film

PUZZLING ! THRILLING MYSTERY . STRANGEST UNSOLVED MYSTERIES OF ALL TIME.

starring Kevin Costner and Robert De Niro. Stack gave the show an air of legitimacy, which was key, as some critics dismissed its examination of cold cases as tabloid television. His presence was the last and maybe the most important thing "Unsolved Mysteries" needed in order to take off.

A mysterious formula

N BC was very happy with the specials, and ordered a weekly series to debut in the fall of 1988. But there were still some growing pains to work through.

By the producers' own admission, the earliest reenactments on the show were rough. Cosgrove and Meurer used the actual people involved in a case whenever possible. While that gave the segments an authentic feel, it also meant that regular people were called upon to act. The results were mixed, to say the least. To solve this problem, Stack would narrate over the scenes, effectively drowning out some of the less effective performances.

The reenactments would prove to be a trademark of the show once producers could afford real actors. But the real secret to the success of "Unsolved Mysteries" was hidden in how it presented its cases. In almost every episode, Cosgrove and Meurer highlighted one eerie, unexplained death and one story of lost love.

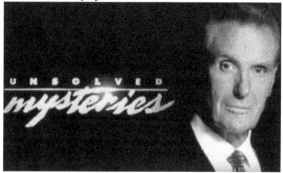

For the other two segments, they'd rotate stories from categories like missing persons, fugitives, amnesia, or fraud. There might also be an update on a previously-aired case. By changing up the stories, the show had something for everyone. But when it came to the paranormal segments, they had at least one vocal critic — Robert Stack.

The host was outspoken about his reluctance to cover paranormal stories, which Cosgrove and Meurer labeled their "ooga booga" material and which sometimes featured very affordable special effects like shining lights in an actor's face or using a projector to depict a ghost. The show went to great lengths to present stories they felt had credibility — they rejected 80 percent of paranormal ideas. But that wasn't enough for Stack, who would sometimes challenge the more fantastic elements of the show. He was less than enthused about doing a Halloween special in 1988 that was devoted entirely to supernatural stories, but NBC insisted. At the time, a syndicated special about Jack the Ripper was about to air, and the network wanted to compete against it. "Unsolved Mysteries" won, but it was a bittersweet victory: That Jack the Ripper special was produced by Cosgrove and Meurer.

It didn't take long for "Unsolved Mysteries" to go from a modest success to a huge hit. By 1990, it was ranked 11th in the ratings out of 131 shows. Up to 30 percent of all viewers watching television during its time slot were tuned in to "Unsolved Mysteries." And at a cost of $375,000 to $700,000 an episode, it was about half as expensive as most hour-long dramas. After all, it didn't cost much to hire unknown actors — unknown at the time, anyway.

Acting suspicious

With multiple reenactments per episode, "Unsolved Mysteries" provided plenty of opportunities for actors looking to get their big break. If you watch classic episodes, you'll probably be able to spot a few performers who went on to greater success.

Matthew McConaughey played a murder victim in a 1992 episode. He later told IMDb that he was "the guy that got shot while mowing my mother's grass." McConaughey went on to say that a viewer tip led to the arrest of the murderer 11 days later. The next year, McConaughey appeared in "Dazed and Confused" as David Wooderson, launching his career as a guy that didn't get shot mowing his mother's grass.

"Curb Your Enthusiasm's Cheryl Hines appeared in a 1997 segment about fugitive Maria Rosa Hernandez. Hines played a mother whose child was attacked by Hernandez.

Daniel Dae Kim, who played Jin-Soo Kwon on the show "Lost," can be seen in an episode playing the brother-in-law of a murder victim named Su-Ya Kim.

Finally, future "Saturday Night Live" cast member Taran Killam played a World War II-era German kid in one memorable segment. Killam had an in, though — his mother's aunt was married to an actor named Robert Stack.

Leaving a tip

I n many of the episodes of "Unsolved Mysteries," Stack is seen in a trench coat standing in front of some appropriately spooky location. Sometimes he appeared in front of a Masonic temple that gave the show a gothic atmosphere. Other times, Stack would stand in front of a phone bank of telephone operators.

This wasn't just for show. During and after a typical episode of the series, roughly 28 operators would field around 1500 calls from viewers, many of whom believed they had information that could lead to the resolution of a case. The show took legitimate tips extremely seriously — so seriously that an FBI agent was often standing by on set in Los Angeles to act on valid information. Representatives from other law enforcement agencies would be on hand if the series was profiling a case from their jurisdiction.

There were a few indicators of a hot tip. Multiple callers describing details in a similar way was a good sign; calls coming from the same region were also regarded as promising.

The show could find resolution quickly: In 1991, a maintenance worker named Becky Granniss was watching "Unsolved Mysteries" when she saw a profile of an alleged killer named Gregory Richard Barker. She thought Barker looked familiar, and then she realized she knew Barker as Alex Graham, a telephone solicitor who worked in her building. Grannis called the show and Barker was arrested just 18 hours later.

Even more impressively, the show was able to help locate Cheryl Holland, a woman from Tennessee who burned down the house of Joe and Mattie Harvey, then killed the couple for their money with help from her common-law husband, Eddie Wooten. Cheryl was their niece. Just 45 minutes after Cheryl's segment aired, she was arrested in Rollingwood, Texas, where she had been hiding out and working at a convenience store.

But not all calls were that helpful. Some people phoned in hoping to talk to Stack and convince him to feature their own mysteries. Producers also looked at viewer mail and used a newspaper clipping service that worked kind of like a pre-internet Google Alert to find stories for the show. The service sent in articles from around the country that featured keywords like "murder," "missing," and "UFO." Cosgrove and Meurer liked stories that had multiple theories or where enough information was present where it seemed like it could be solved.

As you might expect, some people who contacted the show were not necessarily "Unsolved Mysteries" material. One man sent in his mother's lung because he believed she had been murdered and wanted forensic testing performed.

The case files

Throughout its run, "Unsolved Mysteries" profiled well over 1000 cases, and had a high degree of success: Over 340 cases were solved. At one point, the producers estimated that they could solve 60 percent of lost love cases, help locate around 18 percent of the missing heirs they profiled, and even helped capture over half of the fugitives featured. Many of these resolutions were covered in the update segment, which producers said was the most popular among viewers.

The show had many memorable segments — both solved and unsolved — that fans are likely to remember, including:

Cynthia Anderson: Cynthia Anderson was a 20-year-old legal secretary in Toledo, Ohio, who had recurring dreams about a man who entered her house to harm her. She also received harassing phone calls—so many that her employers installed an alarm buzzer on her desk in case there was a problem. On August 4, 1981, Cynthia disappeared from the law office. The door of the office was locked, and her car was still in the parking lot. Police had no leads. But two anonymous phone calls came in where a woman claimed Cynthia was being held in a basement. She's never been found. The most chilling part? The novel left on her desk after her disappearance was open to a page describing an abduction.

The Kecksburg UFO Incident: It's easy to dismiss a UFO sighting by one or two people. But on December 9, 1965, thousands of people in the northeast reported strange lights in the sky. In Kecksburg, Pennsylvania, residents claimed they saw government officials surrounding an *acorn-shaped spacecraft. Was it a meteor? A satellite? Or did the town of Kecksburg have a close encounter? No one knows for sure.*

The Circleville Letters: In 1976, several letters were sent to school bus driver Mary Gillespie of Circleville, Ohio, accusing her of having an affair with the school superintendent. Both Mary and her husband, Ron Gillespie, thought they knew who it was. Ron went out to confront the letter-writer, only to be killed after his car crashed into a tree. Authorities discovered that he had fired his gun before the accident, leading to more questions. The letters didn't stop with Ron's death — in fact, they continued for years, eventually escalating off the page and onto harassing signs posted along Mary's bus route. She ripped one of the signs down one day and discovered a booby trap behind it that would have fired a gun had she pulled the sign down in just the right way. The gun belonged to her brother-in-law, Paul Freshour, who was charged with attempted murder. He was also believed to be the one writing the threatening letters but denied both setting the trap and being the poison penman. Freshour was paroled in 1994 and maintains he didn't write the letters. When "Unsolved Mysteries" was preparing to profile the case in 1993, the production got a postcard warning them to stay away. It was signed "The Circleville Writer."

Craig Williamson: Craig Williamson told his wife Christine he was going on a trip to Colorado Springs, Colorado, to sell tilapia they had raised on their farm in Wisconsin. That was August 28, 1993. On August 30, she spoke to him on the phone. Then he vanished. Christine thought a concussion he had suffered a few weeks prior may have given him amnesia. It wasn't until he was profiled on the show that a viewer recognized him. Actually, the viewer recognized himself. Craig was watching "Unsolved Mysteries" when his face appeared onscreen. He was living in Key West, Florida, and claimed he had been mugged, lost his memory, and started a new life there. He reunited with Christine, but because he said he couldn't remember anything, they got divorced. Solved? Kinda. He was found — but did he really have amnesia?

PUZZLING ! THRILLING MYSTERY . STRANGEST UNSOLVED MYSTERIES OF ALL TIME.

The Lucky Choir: Everyone in the church choir at West End Baptist Church in Beatrice, Nebraska, knew better than to arrive late for practice. The choir director, Martha Paul, was extremely punctual and expected the same of her performers. They were all due at 7:25 p.m. But on March 1, 1950, all 15 members were late for various personal reasons ranging from car problems to homework. At exactly 7:27 p.m., the church exploded. The pastor, Walter Klempl, had turned on the heat earlier that afternoon not knowing there was an issue that could lead to a gas explosion. For the 1990 segment, producers of "Unsolved Mysteries" found a church in Unadilla, Nebraska, that was due to be demolished and blew it up. The resulting fireball was said to have reached a quarter-mile into the air.

Mystery solved

"Unsolved Mysteries" kept the spooky music humming for nine seasons before being canceled by NBC in 1997. But Stack didn't hang up his trench coat for long. The show was picked up by CBS, where it aired for two more seasons. When CBS declined to renew it, it found yet another home on Lifetime, where it aired through 2002.

When Robert Stack passed away in May 2003 at the age of 84, that seemed to be the end. But the show returned in 2008 on Spike TV with actor Dennis Farina as host. Farina, who was once a Chicago police officer, stuck with the show through 2010.

Classic episodes have been available on streaming services like Amazon Prime, sometimes with updates, which Cosgrove and Meurer have said are mandatory if a person featured in a segment has been released from prison. Other times, they've deleted segments if the statute of limitations has expired or if the law enforcement agency handling the case asked them to remove it. Unsolved Mysteries was recently revived again, both as a podcast and as a series for Netflix.

So why do we keep coming back to a show about unexplained disappearances, strange alien sightings, and amnesia? It's simple: "Unsolved Mysteries" was interactive television. People watched because they never knew if they'd see a suspect or missing person just around the corner. They enjoyed the ambiguity, and they knew that even if the show didn't offer a resolution for one case, they'd be able to wrap up another. It was scary without being graphic. It was emotional without being exploitative. And it had Robert Stack, who could make anything—even little green men — sound plausible.

It's unknown if Stack had a favorite segment, but if he did, it might have been the one where the show profiled a famous lawman who battled the infamous Al Capone before searching for a serial killer in 1930s Cleveland. His name? Eliot Ness.

PART -2
Campsite Killer: The Unsolved Mystery of Lake Bodom Murders

The worst night of Neil Wilhelm Gustafsson's life is one he doesn't remember. On June 4, 1960, Gustafsson, then 18, at a camp in Esperanto, Finland, to spend time with his friends.

The worst night of Neil Wilhelm Gustafsson's life is one he doesn't remember. On June 4, 1960, Gustafsson, then 17, set out for a camp in the town of Espe, Finland, to spend time with his friends. The group included Seppo Antero Boisman; Boseman's girlfriend, Anja Tulikki Maki; And Gustafsson's girlfriend, Myla Irmeli Buzzerklund. The teenagers set up a single tent on the shores of Lake Bodom and began a night of socialization and drinking. At one point in the evening they retired to the tent.

The next morning, on a bird-watching expedition, two travelers spotted the tent in the distance through the campgrounds. They weren't so close to seeing many details, but it was clear that the tent was torn and cut. Nearby, a blonde haired man was seen walking away from the camp site.

The boys continued, obviously thinking a little bit of it. Later in the morning, a local passed by the tent and was close enough to see a startled *sight. Outside the tent, Gustafsson and Brazarklund were bloodied and stingy (according to some accounts, Bazarklund was partially hidden inside the tent fabric). Authorities found Boisman and Maki inside, their bodies with knife mold and bruises that corresponded to bullying. Borkland, Boisman and Maki died. Only Gustafsson survived the attack. When police asked him what had happened, he could only tell that a shadow group dressed in bright red-eyed black had appeared and had mischievously attacked the group.*

As months and years went by, the police were unable to gather any additional information from the lone survivor of this horrific incident. It was a sensitive event that became common sense among the inhabitants of Finland. Everyone knew about the Lake Bodom murder and how the authorities were unable to identify the culprit. The children were warned that the killer was still hiding if it did not go after dark.

In March 2004, everything changed. Nearly half a century later, DNA evidence led lawyers to suspect that they claimed the murder was intentional. The case was unavailable to forensic scientists in 1960.

Their suspect was Neil Gustafson.

Investigators did not suspect Gustafson at the time of the murder. When Finnish police arrived at the crime scene, his condition was critical, with a broken jaw, bruises and a concussion. He could not remember anything but the description of a supernatural person, who seemed to have been born in a state of shock.

Police tried to gather what was transported on the basis of physical evidence. On June 4, the group arrived on a motorcycle near Lake Bodom, a popular camping and fishing site about 14 miles from Helsinki. The bikes were still there when authorities arrived, but the keys were missing. Gustafson's shoes were also thought to have been lost, until investigators removed them about a mile and a half from their camp site. No murder weapon was found at the scene.

The most intriguing observation was how the killer started the attack. The teenagers probably threw knives while they were in the tent and the killers fell to the shelter for stabbing them. Gustafson was found at the top of the tent. According to some versions, it was Bozorklund, which means he either crawled out of the tent or his body must have moved between the time of the attack and the arrival of the police.

IN MOST CASES THE SCENE would have become mysterious. Investigators, however, failed to fully secure the area and tightened their own work by inviting search teams to find clues. Their assistance meant the crime scene was disrupted, making it difficult to assess for footprints or other evidence.

With the lack of physical evidence, the possibility of finding a resolution did not seem promising. No arrests were made, and only a handful of suspects were released in the years that followed. Interested was Carl Valdemar Gilstrom, who ran a kiosk business on the campground and was known as a very fickle man who often issued issues with the campers, probably because of the camp. It was said that Jelstrom still cut the tent stains and even threw stones at the visitors if he was in a particularly bad mood. In the wake of the campfire surrounding the crime, some people believed that Gilstrom had simply robbed and brutally humiliated Gustafson's party.

This theory gained momentum when Gailstrom died by suicide in 19 theory. Presumably, he confessed to the murder before he died. As disgusting as it seemed, the police announced that Jailstrom could not commit the crime. According to his wife, he was in bed with her on the night of the attack (although some think it was forcibly alibi). The motive for the confession was false, although it is not clear how it prompted Gailstrom to take responsibility for the killings.

There were other leaders of the police as well. There was Paulie Luoma, who was said to be in the vicinity of the camp, but her alibi was confirmed to be staying that night in another town. But no one else linked him to the crime, and police thought it was nothing more than prisonhouse arrogance.

Unfortunately there was more reason to think another suspect named Hans Asman was suspicious. A doctor named Jorma Polo insisted that at one point in the murder, Sky came to Helsinki Surgical Hospital with dirt under his nails and blood on his clothes. The English language accounts of the crime do not specify why he sought treatment. But when the police saw it, they saw that there was a believable alibi in the sky.

It seemed that no one could be kept at the scene. There was no one but the man who came out alive.

For decades, the Lake Bodom mystery had faded. Meanwhile, DNA testing was growing into an effective method of re-examination in both current and cold cases, the first being used in the 1980s. In Finland, however, with only a single forensic lab serving the entire country, there was little bandwidth to focus on the old investigation.

Forensic scientists at the country's National Investigation Bureau Crime Lab tested the shoes and found blood from the victims. Notably, the shoes themselves were missing any blood from Gustafson. How he could be attacked with others, yet only had his DNA in his shoes, was wondered. Authorities believe the explanation was that he carried out the attack himself, then somehow threw off his shoes before attacking himself as if he had been frustrated by a third party.

Investigators theorized that Guptafson may have been forced to kill the three because of some violence. In fact, the man who was stationed at a nearby camp on the eve of the murder testified in court that he saw

Gustafsson and Boisman in intense debate, making Gustafsson appear heavily organized. Presumably, investigators thought Buzzerklund had rejected his advance. Or Gustafson believed that Boysman was on his way. This will explain why Buzzerklund was stabbed and hit with a higher frequency than the others. Police speculate that Gustafson was exiled from the tent, possibly after a boxing fight with Boisman, who was thrown with a broken jaw. Then he returned in anger,

The story of the Espur district prosecutor had enough faith to bring charges against Gustafson, with the possibility of life in prison if convicted. In protest of his innocence, his lawyer, Rita Leppiniemi, argued that Gustafson's blood was inside the tent and that pushing a broken jaw into Boysman's hand did not leave him in a position to violently kill three people. Leppinemi also criticized the testimony of an eyewitness to the camp, who for 45 years was silent about the fight in the interview for reasons determined to be the cause of a fight and could not remember certain details.

During the 2005 trial, a police officer named Marku Tuminen claimed that Gustafson had clarified his case after his arrest, saying "what has been done has been done," predicting that he would receive 15 years for the crime. Gustafson, however, denies this, and the story he has been telling for decades is stuck in the same way. He couldn't remember anything other than going fishing with Boisman and there was no reason for it.

The court eventually discovered that there was not enough evidence to convict Gustafson, noting that too much time had elapsed to compile an accurate picture of the incident. Gustafson was released.

Almost 100 years have passed since the June 1960 incident, but no answer seems to have come. The crime is still a part of Finnish folklore. This inspired a heavy metal band to dub the children of Bodom; The band even released a beer made of water from the lake. Some people in Finland have tried to sue Gustafsson, claiming that he did not inadvertently remember anything as a confession. If he can't remember what happened, how did he know he didn't do it? But this kind of argument is not for the cleanliness of the courtroom.

Another question is why Gustafson's shoes were kept so far from the camp site. If he takes them to sleep, why not put them near the tabernacle? Who was that golden light when the boys later saw the crime scene go away from them? (The sky was weird; it's not clear what color Gustafson's hair was at the time of the attack.) And if Gustafson somehow worked with nerves to stab himself in a stage attack, why didn't the blood trail get there? Was the knife deposited or hidden?

The only clue surrounding the murder is that someone managed to kill three people on the shores of Lake Bodom. Whether it's men, women, teams or anything with bright red eyes they seem to have removed it.

PART- 3
Leading theories about D.B. Cooper and 30 other unsolved mysteries

Thanks to the American fascination with confounding unsolved cases, mystery is among the most popular genres of books, movies, and television. From heists and capers to murders and robberies, the world's greatest unsolved mysteries spark media frenzies that grab headlines around the globe. Some cases compel so much public intrigue that the facts and theories

surrounding them become the basis of books, movies, plays, and documentaries decades or even centuries after the cases go cold.

The internet breathed new life into many of the world's great unsolved mysteries, giving amateur detectives and self-directed sleuths the tools they needed to scrounge for new clues and fresh leads long after official authorities stopped searching for answers. Along the way, public fascination inevitably led to wild speculation, fantastical theories, and a hazy blur between facts as they actually happened and outrageous rumors that the media and public adopt as reality.

Stacker used a variety of sources to summarize 31 of the most enduring and perplexing unsolved mysteries, from grisly murders and ghost ships to great escapes and entire colonies of people disappearing without a trace. In some cases, the information came from law enforcement agencies like the Federal Bureau of Investigation, who have been working directly on solving the case the whole time. Other times, the source material was news reports surrounding new developments in the cases. Occasionally, organizations or individuals like authors or amateur detectives came up with the best information after dedicating years or even decades to studying and researching these baffling and unsolved scenarios on their own.

If the facts and fictions surrounding the most salacious and unbelievably true whodunits pique your interest and stir your passions, you are not alone. Keep reading to learn about some of the world's greatest unsolved mysteries and the leading theories about what really happened.

On Nov. 24, 1971, a man in a business suit calling himself Dan Cooper (the media invented the popularized "D.B.") boarded a plane from Portland to Seattle, told a stewardess he had a bomb, and showed her a briefcase with a device inside that convinced her it was real. He then demanded $200,000 and four parachutes, which the crew gave him, and when the plane landed, he released the passengers but held some crew hostage for his second demand—a flight to Mexico. When that plane was in the air, "Cooper" astonished the crew by jumping out of it into the night sky. He was never seen again. The case has baffled the FBI and the public ever *since. The FBI closed the case in 2016, but there is still plenty of speculation that far exceeds the popular assumption that Cooper died during the jump that would have landed him in a remote wilderness. Some say Cooper was actually a former Army helicopter pilot named Robert Rack straw who died in July 2019, while another theory revolves around one Lynn Doyle Cooper whose niece came forward in 2011 to say her late uncle plotted the hijacking at a family gathering in 1971.*

Alcatraz escapees

O n June 12, 1962, a headcount at Alcatraz—the most secure, remote prison in America—revealed that three inmates were missing. In their beds were dummies fashioned out of plaster and human hair, which fooled the guards the night before—all part of an ingenious and elaborate

ruse that included life vests and rafts made from raincoat rubber. Despite one of the most exhaustive investigations in the FBI's history and endless public speculation, no one knows the fate of Frank Morris and brothers John and Clarence

Anglin to this day, although authorities believe they likely died in the treacherous waters of the San Francisco Bay.

The Sims Family

In 1966, the grisly murder of a prominent family rocked Tallahassee, Florida, when 17-year-old Norma Jeannette Sims returned home from a babysitting gig to find her mother, father, and 12-year-old sister bound, gagged, shot, and stabbed to death. The case, which changed the previously quiet community forever—Ted Bundy would commit his most infamous murders at a Florida State University sorority house in the city in 1978—remains unsolved. Although a local pastor was long suspected, Leon County Sheriff Larry Campbell, who was a 24-year-old deputy and early responder that night, has said he knows of two suspects who he believes did it, although he refuses to name them to this day.

Jack the Ripper

The mysterious man known as Jack the Ripper, who terrorized the Whitechapel district of London in 1888, is still the most famous serial killer in history. According to Science magazine, forensic analysts published genetic analysis evidence in 2019 that could finally reveal the long-anonymous murderer who

killed and mutilated London prostitutes so long ago. They believe Jack the Ripper was a 23-year-old Polish barber named Aaron Kosminski, one of the main suspects at the time of the murders, though evidence isn't quite strong enough to mark the case officially closed.

Jimmy Hoffa

M ore than a dozen people have claimed to have killed Jimmy Hoffa since the powerful Teamsters union boss went missing in 1975 and was listed as "presumed dead" in 1982. Most recently, Martin Scorsese's blockbuster "The Irishman" stoked new interest in a credible claim made by the movie's namesake, mafia hitman Frank Sheeran. Even the skeptics who doubt Sheeran's claim believe that if it wasn't him, it was a different killer for the Bufalino crime family, with which both Sheeran and Hoffa were long associated.

Amelia Earhart

A viation pioneer, feminist icon, and American hero Amelia Earhart made her final radio transmission on July 2, 1937, when she and her navigator disappeared while attempting to circle the globe across 30,000 miles in an airplane. In the decades since, there has been no shortage of speculation, with some theories backed up by fairly compelling evidence, including one that she was captured by the Japanese military and another that she was marooned and lived on a remote Pacific island. The most likely and widely believed scenario, however, is that she crashed during bad weather and sank in the vast Pacific Ocean near where her last broadcast was transmitted.

Lizzie Borden

Few murder mysteries have remained ingrained in the public imagination longer or more deeply than the 1892 axe murder of upper-crust Massachusetts residents Andrew and Abby Borden. Andrew's daughter Lizzie Borden was 32 and unmarried (a minor scandal for the upper class at that time) when she immediately became the main and only suspect, only to be acquitted a year later in 1893. Alternate theories have been pitched for more than a century, but Lizzie—who was home at the time and had plenty of motives—remains the only true suspect with any real evidence pointing to her as the killer.

The Phantom Barber

*I**n 1942, one of the strangest unsolved crime sprees*

understandably terrified the town of Pascagoula, Mississippi, when a man dubbed "The Phantom Barber" broke into homes, cut locks of hair off women and children, and left without stealing anything or otherwise harming anyone. Fifty-seven-year-old William Dolan was soon arrested and convicted—he had human hair in his home, and some victims were likely incapacitated with chloroform while he was a chemist by trade. His sentence, however, was

33

later suspended when he passed a lie detector test and police were accused of mishandling the case in a rush to find a suspect. He remains, however, the only credible suspect.

The Mary Celeste

The ship *Mary Celeste* left New York City for Genoa, Italy, in 1872, only to be discovered at sea partially flooded and missing a lifeboat, but otherwise intact, seaworthy, packed with supplies, and empty. The disappearance of the 10 people on board remains one of history's greatest maritime mysteries. Books, plays, and movies were written about the many theories surrounding the ghost ship, including pirate takeovers, mutiny, waterspouts, sea monsters, and deadly rampages by former slaves. In 2007, however, *Smithsonian* magazine outlined exhaustive research that revealed the most likely scenario: Coal dust fouled the boat's pumps, which led the captain to order the crew and passengers to abandon ship in the belief that he was closer to land than he really was.

Lost Colony of Roanoke

T*he Lost Colony of Roanoke, founded in present-day North Carolina in 1587 and discovered empty in 1590, is the oldest mystery in*

American history, considering it took place two decades before the founding of Jamestown. Volumes have been written about what might have happened to the 100-plus English settlers who lived there, including massacres by Indians or the Spanish, enslavement, starvation, cannibalism, and failed attempts to return to England. In 2018, however, National Geographic reported on compelling research that revealed the most likely scenario: The desperate colonists assimilated into a local Native American tribe.

Area 51

Officially named the Nevada Test and Training Range at Groom Lake, Area 51 is a highly secure, highly secretive Air Force training range in southern Nevada—and the epicenter of America's UFO/alien conspiracy theory counterculture since the 1950s. Since rumors of a UFO crash near Roswell, New Mexico, first emerged in 1947, the Air Force has investigated thousands of reports of UFOs

at or near Area 51. The most likely scenario, according to Time magazine, is that civilians and military personnel alike witnessed experimental aircraft being tested there and mistook them for alien spacecraft, and government secrecy went a long way in fueling alien fever.

The Boston art heist

I n 1990, two men dressed as policemen entered Boston's Isabella Stewart Gardner Museum, tied up the guards, and stole 13 famous works of art worth $500 million in what remains the world's largest unsolved art heist. Nearly 30 years later, in 2018,

authorities renewed a $10 million reward, which generated an avalanche of tips and theories that included a mafia heist, the Irish Republican Army, rock musicians turned museum robbers, and security guards as part of an inside job. Most credibly, the FBI believes that a Mid-Atlantic crime ring led by a man who was killed in a 1991 gang war pulled off the world's greatest unsolved art heist.

The Zodiac Killer

The Zodiac Killer, a still-unidentified serial murderer who terrorized Northern California in the 1960s and '70s, got his name from the taunting letters, ciphers, and cryptograms he sent authorities and newspapers during his reign of terror. Several people have credibly claimed either to have been the Zodiac Killer or to have known who he was, but the most likely suspect is Arthur Leigh Allen, who true crime author Robert Graysmith convincingly argued was the Zodiac Killer in two separate books on the subject. Allen died in 1992.

Bugsy Siegel

B enjamin "Bugsy" Siegel, America's first celebrity mobster, was instrumental in transforming Las Vegas into a destination city, one that was controlled and bankrolled by the Mafia. Siegel was shot to death in Southern California on June 20, 1947, shortly after his Flamingo Hotel opened on the Las Vegas strip. Although his murder remains unsolved, some believe that Siegel's childhood friend and gangster mentor Meyer Lansky set up the assassination in response to disputes about how Siegel was spending money. Siegel and Lansky were portrayed as Moe Greene and Hyman Roth in "The Godfather" movie franchise.

Harry Houdini

H*arry Houdini died in 1926 at 52, and to this day, the master showman's name is still associated with great escapes or disappearing*

acts. Throughout his career, Houdini upped the ante in pulling off seemingly impossible escapes in increasingly dangerous and outlandish situations. He allowed a medical student to punch him in the stomach during one show, something the famously fit magician and escape artist was known to do, and it was long believed that his mysterious death was the result of internal injuries *stemming from the punch. Medical professionals now believe, however, that the Hungarian immigrant born Erik Weisz more likely succumbed to appendicitis and sepsis, which would have killed him anyway, belly punch or no belly punch.*

Judge Joseph F. Crater

J oseph Force Crater was a rising star in the corrupt world of New York's Tammany Hall Democratic politics and a

state Supreme Court judge when he got into a taxi and vanished without a trace in the summer of 1930. His disappearance remains one of the most high-profile, thoroughly investigated, nearly completely lead-less, and salacious mysteries in American history—the mountains of tips that poured in included rumors of philandering with showgirls, massive political bribes, mob connections, and shady insurance dealings. The people most closely associated with the case believe that he likely knew too much about the inner workings of Tammany

Hall and its mobbed-up associates and that Judge Crater received the same treatment that Jimmy Hoffa would receive decades later.

Elizabeth Short

Twenty-two-year-old aspiring actress Elizabeth Short, famously dubbed "Black Dahlia" by the media, was found dead and expertly

dismembered on a Los Angeles street in 1947. The murder sparked a whirlwind of public interest and the mystery still tantalizes to this day. Although it never went anywhere, the most promising lead at the time pointed to a group of university medical students who would have been adept at dissecting bodies as cleanly as the Black Dahlia's had been.

Billy the Kid

*I*t was long believed that Billy the Kid, the most famous outlaw in Old West history, was killed by lawman Pat Garrett

—the problem, however, is that the account that cemented that story in the public consciousness was written by Garrett himself. In the ensuing years, countless historians, amateur detectives, and plenty of imposter Billy the Kids have insisted that Billy escaped Garrett's wrath that day in 1881 and continued his remarkable life on the run in disguise. In 1990, "Young Guns II" portrayed Billy as having lived to old age into the 20th century. Most of the facts, however, confirm that Billy the Kid's short, violent life probably did end at the barrel of Pat Garrett's pistol.

Tupac Shakur

What's most unbelievable about the brazen and highly public drive-by shooting murder of Tupac Shakur on the crowded Las Vegas strip in 1996 is that it still hasn't been solved.

A central figure in the East Coast/West Coast rap beef, Shakur had deep gang ties. He was riding in the car with the career criminal and record producer Marion "Suge" Knight when he was killed and his list of avowed and dangerous enemies was as long as his lengthy rap sheet. Although the media firestorm that ensued included speculation that his killers were corrupt Los Angeles police officers or East Coast rivals sent by Sean "Diddy" Combs, it's most likely that he was killed by a crew of rival gang members who he fought in a casino earlier that evening, including Orlando "Baby Lane" Anderson, a Crip gang member who was murdered himself at the age of 23.

Christopher 'Biggie Smalls' Wallace

A lmost exactly six months after Tupac Shakur was gunned down, his East Coast arch-rival Christopher Wallace (better known as the

Notorious B.I.G.) was murdered in Los Angeles, bringing to a close the violent cross-country rivalry that had dominated the 1990s rap world and enthralled the media and the public. Astonishingly, the Biggie Smalls murder also remains unsolved, and Wallace's music and lifestyle similarly left no shortage of suspects with means and motive. Although unfounded speculation fueled rumors that police or the FBI were complicit in the murders of both men—who were once close friends—most fingers point to Death Row Records CEO Suge Knight as having orchestrated the murder of Wallace as revenge for the killing of Tupac.

JonBenét Ramsey

W hen a six-y ear-old child beauty queen was brutally killed in her Colorado home in 1996, it seemed that everyone in America suddenly knew the name JonBenét Ramsey. Her parents were the original suspects, followed later by her brother, but DNA evidence ruled them out. More than a quarter-century later, the world still asks, "who killed JonBenét?" In 2019, Rolling Stone reported on compelling evidence that Gary Oliva, a convicted pedophile and longtime suspect, actually, and perhaps accidentally, committed the murder.

Edgar Allan Poe

I t's fitting that Edgar Allan Poe, long known as the master of morbid prose, died under circumstances so mysterious

that as many as nine theories still surround his unexplained death, which occurred as Poe writhed in a fit of delirium in 1849. The leading theories include murder, alcohol *withdrawal, a beating, rabies, heavy metal poisoning, and carbon monoxide poisoning. According to Smithsonian Magazine, however, it was probably something much less sinister like the flu or a related illness.*

Ambrose Bierce

I n 1913, the 71-year-old Ambrose Bierce, a famous writer and Civil War veteran, left on horseback to cover the Mexican Revolutionary War and

was never seen again.

Theories about his death included him dying in battle, defecting to the army of Pancho Villa, and being kidnapped and killed by Federales. Most likely, however, he was caught by Mexican military authorities who assumed he was a spy and, not able to speak Spanish, was summarily executed after being unable to answer their questions.

PRABIR RAICHAUDHURI

Annie McCarrick

*L*ong Island, New York native Annie McCarrick was living in Ireland when she suddenly vanished in 1993 and, despite a massive manhunt, no trace of her was ever found. She was one of several women who disappeared in the 1990s in an area dubbed Ireland's "Vanishing Triangle." The area was the hunting ground of a serial killer long believed to be convicted rapist Larry Murphy, and McCarrick is thought to be one of his victims.

Walter Collins

T*he 2008 Angelina Jolie and Clint Eastwood movie "Changeling"
chronicles the real-life story of Christine Collins, whose nine-year-old
son, Walter, went missing in*

*1928. The LAPD then
returned to her a different, older boy who turned out to be a willing imposter
named Arthur Hutchins Jr., who later admitted to concocting the scheme to*

escape an abusive household. When Collins protested, she was involuntarily committed to a mental hospital and was later exonerated. It has long been believed, but never proven, that the real Walter Collins was one victim of serial killers Gordon Stewart Northcott and his mother Sarah Louise Northcott, who killed little boys in the area.

Paula Jean Welden

P aula Jean Welden is the most famous of five people of all ages and genders who vanished from the small town of Bennington, Vermont,

between 1945 and 1950. After the young college student disappeared in a wooded area, fear and gossip gripped the community. It's likely that an unnamed young man originally suspected and questioned by police was a serial killer, but local cops bungled the case, which led to the formation of the Vermont State Police.

Tylenol poisonings

T amper-resistant packaging on modern medicine directly results from one incident, which terrified the nation, baffled law enforcement, and

threatened the country's supply of food and drugs: the Tylenol poisonings. In 1982, a still-unknown assailant spiked Tylenol capsules with deadly cyanide, leading to the deaths of several people in the Chicago area and launching one of the most significant law enforcement investigations in modern history. A man named James William Lewis was convicted of extortion for mailing a ransom letter to Johnson & Johnson demanding money for an end to the poisonings, and although he couldn't be pinned to the actual act, many of the lead investigators still believe he was the perpetrator.

Flannan Isles Lighthouse

S *pooky, desolate, and remote, the Flannan Isles Lighthouse in Scotland had long been the subject of paranormal stories and superstitions. It didn't help when an arriving ship found the lighthouse*

mysteriously empty with no trace of all three lighthouse keepers in December 1900. Local lore fueled wild speculation about malignant apparitions, sea creatures, and murder stoked by desolation-induced madness. Terrible weather had plagued the surrounding seas, and it's most likely that the three men had gone down to the base of the lighthouse to secure a supply crate to mooring ropes to haul the crate up, and were swept away by a massive rogue wave.

Canva The Millbrook twins

On March 18, 1990, the 15-year-old twin sisters Dannette and Jeannette Millbrook disappeared without a trace in Augusta,

Georgia. Their disappearance remains the only case of missing twins to remain unsolved in the United States. Georgia police dismissed them as runaways and put little effort into finding the twins in the days and years following their disappearance, prompting accusations of racial bias from the Millbrook family and their many supporters. Recently, new media attention has brought their plight back into the spotlight, leading to new digging by professional and amateur investigators alike, many of whom believe they fell victim to serial killer Joseph Patrick Washington, who operated in that area at that time.

Marilyn Sheppard

The brutal 1954 bludgeoning death of Marilyn Sheppard and the controversial conviction of her husband, Dr. Sam Sheppard is the most enduring murder mystery in Cleveland history and was the basis of the TV show and movie "The Fugitive." Dr. Sheppard's conviction was overturned in 1966 and he died in 1970. Today, his descendants and the investigators who still fixate on the sensational case believe the real killer

was   Richard Eberling, a convicted murderer and window washer at the Sheppard home.

Bob Crane

In 1978, the nation was stunned when "Hogan's Heroes" star Bob Crane was found brutally murdered in his Arizona home. Police there are believed to have mishandled the case from the beginning and the murder remains unsolved, but the incident has continued to fascinate the public and gnaw at Crane's surviving family. It's believed that John Carpenter, a longtime friend of Crane's who was arrested, tried, and acquitted in 1994 due to botched forensic evidence, is guilty of the murder.

| ©-2021, Prabir Rai Chaudhuri .

Don't miss out!

Visit the website below and you can sign up to receive emails whenever Prabir RaiChaudhuri publishes a new book. There's no charge and no obligation.

https://books2read.com/r/B-A-ZLCT-SHPAC

BOOKS 2 READ

Connecting independent readers to independent writers.

Did you love *Puzzling ! Thrilling Mystery . Strangest Unsolved Mysteries of All Time.*? Then you should read *Fantasy-Fun-Moral ; Selected short stories for kids with moral*[1] by Prabir RaiChaudhuri!

Short children's stories to daydream. Fairy tales, Short stories with moral, English moral stories

The short children's stories of this book are designed to awaken the imagination and the restless mind of children. They are short stories full of values, which review each of the morals to adapt to our times and thus serve as an educational resource to transmit values to children.

Its length is designed to quickly capture the child's attention , and in a few lines the beginning, middle and end that any story requires are developed. All this keeping the child attentive to its end. They are short children's stories perfect for bedtime, a moment that parents should take

1. https://books2read.com/u/m0vkgP

2. https://books2read.com/u/m0vkgP

advantage of to enjoy our children and affectively transmit different teachings and values that they will later apply to their daily lives.Traditional tales that never go out of styleBut in this book we also really like traditions, that's why we bring the traditional and popular stories of always, the ones we all know and with which we have grown up: stories like Little Red Riding Hood , The Three Little Pigs , and many others which already live forever in our memory, and that we like to tell children so much.

In some cases we also incorporate more friendly versions of these stories, adapted to our times, where the big bad wolf is not as fierce as they paint it, and where fairy princesses do not need to be saved by princes , because girls are also enough to fight against the bad guys of the story .

Be that as it may, we invite you to enjoy the great variety of stories that we have in the pages of this book. Enjoy reading together, encourage the habit of reading in children, something that will inadvertently help them in their educational development. You will see how the task of reading, writing, and even spelling becomes easier for them, which they will assimilate without even realizing it.

The power of children's stories is infinite, you just have to give wings to the imagination and let it fly along with the pages of this book !

CONTENTSThe story of "Rhino's Diet", "The Princess and the Pea", "THE HARE AND THE TORTOISE", "The grasshopper and the ant", "The cicada and the ant", "The Town Musicians of Bremen", "The story of Sinbad the sailor", "Tale of Goldilocks", "Goldilocks and the Three Bears", "Children's story Tom Thumb", "The Red Shoes", "The sleeping beauty , who slept and slept", "THE THREE LITTLE PIGS", "The smug rat", "Little Red Riding Hood, classic tale", "Story The jumping dwarf (Rumpelstiltskin)", "The Pied Piper of Hamelin", "The seven little kids", "Hansel and Gretel story".

Read more at https://www.manusherbhasha.com/.

Also by Prabir RaiChaudhuri

Fantasy-Fun-Moral ; Selected short stories for kids with moral
Puzzling ! Thrilling Mystery . Strangest Unsolved Mysteries of All Time.
Manga, Anime sketch, drawing, coloring techniques

Watch for more at https://www.manusherbhasha.com/.

About the Author

Prabir Rai Chaudhuri – Born in Kolkata (India) -1975.

Completing higher education from two different universities – University of Calcutta and Jadavpur University. From his young days he decided to teach children and orphan students because in those days , where he lived that time the proper education resources were very limited. He offered his service of teaching and other social activities voluntary with no cost .But doing all these he faced some real need of money.In his life he worked in different sectors and entertained with the different lifestyle of the people , lights , sounds, pain and happyness, loss and success and enriched with those memories that helps him to write . Life is drawn in his pen like a picture with multiple shadow and colors.

He lived in Taki – a rural and heritage city that time. Struggling from his childhood with many issues – mainly the finance ,though he never gave up serving his social responsibilities .

He believes " Honesty and Truth only wins and wins every time" , he is not the person to give it up. Fighting the hurdles and coming back with new things , finding newer way to live have become the life of him. Struggling , and living with people who suffer everyday enriched his experience , diversified his ability to look an issue with multiple angle. Fun and tear , hope and frustration , cruelty and love are the part of the life . and The Children is our future. They should live better with full of happiness . Keep reading his books which full of exclusivity and every time something new is waiting for you that must enrich your lifestyle.

Read more at https://www.manusherbhasha.com/.

About the Publisher